THE SORCERER'S APPRENTICE

Retold by Fiona Chandler

Illustrated by
Poly Bernatene

Reading Consultant: Alison Kelly
Roehampton University

Contents

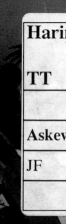

Chapter 1

A task for Max

Max had spent all morning cleaning the sorcerer's workshop – and he still hadn't finished.

Wash this...
Polish that... I'm
fed up with it.

"How will I ever learn to be a sorcerer like Sticklewick?" he moaned. "He never lets me do any magic."

Just then, Max heard footsteps on the stone staircase. "Uh-oh, that's him! Back to work."

4

A moment later, Sticklewick
appeared. "Max, I have to go
into town," he announced,
waving a long shopping list.

"I used the last of the dragons' eggs yesterday and we're out of goblins' toenails."

Max was astonished. Sticklewick had never left him alone in the castle before.

Yippee! A free afternoon!

"I can explore the dungeons and swim in the moat," he thought. "Or just sit in the sun and do nothing at all."

"There's plenty to do while I'm out," Sticklewick went on. "For a start, this floor could do with a good scrub."

Look! I've just stepped on a toadstool.

"But fill up the water tank first. It's almost empty."

8

Max groaned. It always took hours to fetch enough water to fill the tank. And it was such hard work.

"Oh, and one more thing,"
Sticklewick added.
"Don't try any spells!"
He frowned.

"Or I'll... I'll turn you into a
tadpole," he threatened, his
bushy eyebrows bristling.

With that, there was a flash of light and a puff of purple smoke. The sorcerer was gone.

Chapter 2

Max's plan

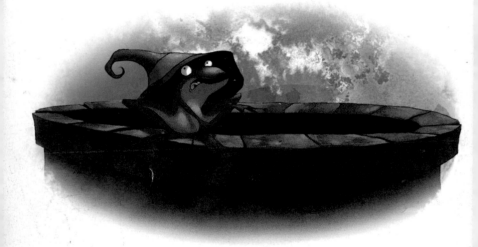

"Well, don't just stand there!" croaked a little voice. "You have work to do." It was Tabitha, Sticklewick's toad.

"Oh, hop it!" said Max, crossly. "I've been working all morning. I need a rest first."

"There's no need to be rude," said Tabitha, hopping onto a broomstick.

13

Max didn't reply. Seeing Tabitha perched on the broom had given him a brilliant idea.

Last week, Sticklewick had cast a spell on a broomstick. It had come to life and done everything the sorcerer asked.

14

"I'm sure I can remember the words," Max thought, concentrating.

How hard can it be?

"You're up to something," said Tabitha. "You'd better not try any spells. You heard what Sticklewick said."

"Don't be such a spoilsport," said Max. "What harm can it do? Anyway, he won't know."

16

Max closed his eyes and thought for a moment. Taking a deep breath, he said the magic words...

Root and branch of old oak tree, bring this broom to life for me!

All at once, the broom began to twitch. It shook and it shuddered, then... slowly... it grew two skinny arms and two skinny legs.

Wow! I did it!

"Now," Max ordered the broom, "fetch me some water. And be quick about it!"

18

The broom ran off. In no
time, Max heard it coming
tap-tap-tap down the steps. It
poured the water into the tank
and set off for more.

Feeling very pleased with himself, Max flopped down in the sorcerer's chair. "Time for a snooze," he yawned.

Soon, he was fast asleep.

ZZZZZZZ

Chapter 3

Trouble ahead

Max woke up to find Tabitha hopping on his lap. "What is it?" he mumbled, sleepily.

"Quick!" croaked Tabitha.
"The tank is overflowing and
the broom won't stop!"

Max jumped to his feet. Water
was sloshing over the sides of
the tank... and the broom was
clattering down the steps again.

22

"Stop!" he shouted. "That's enough!" But the broom took no notice. Streams of water poured across the floor.

"Great stuttering sorcerers, just say the spell!" begged Tabitha.

"What spell?" asked Max, puzzled. Then he remembered. Of course! He needed a spell to make the broom stop.

"Oh no," he groaned. "I... um... I don't think I actually know it."

Oh boy!

By now, the water was ankle deep. And still the broom was fetching more.

"I know!" cried Max, splashing across the floor. "I'll look in Sticklewick's spell book. Let's see..."

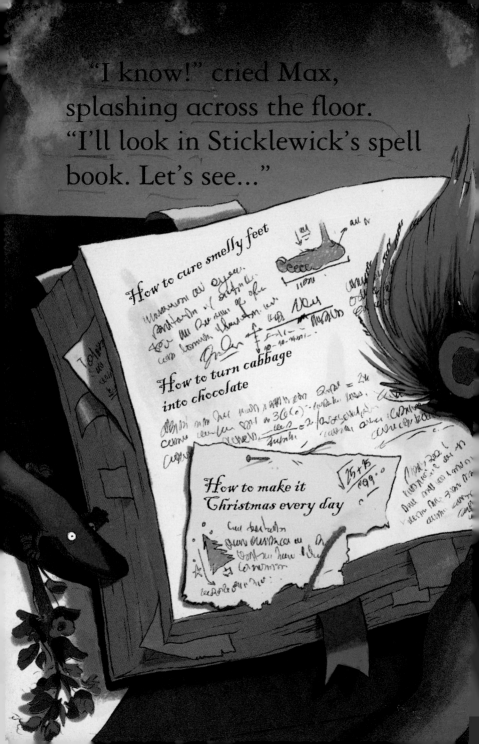

How to cure smelly feet

How to turn cabbage into chocolate

How to make it Christmas every day

How to make pigs fly

How to turn a frog
into a prince

How to disappear in a
puff of smoke

Max flicked through
page after page.

27

"This is hopeless," he wailed.
"There are thousands of spells
here. I'll *never* find the right
one. What am I going to do?"

"You could chop the broom
up," said Tabitha, helpfully.

"Good thinking!" said Max. He grabbed a hatchet, lifted it high above his head and swung it down hard.

With a loud CRACK, the broomstick split in two.

Chapter 4

Double trouble

"That was close," said Max, with a sigh of relief. "Thanks Tabitha, you're brilliant! Tabitha? What's wrong?"

"Look at the broom!"

Max's eyes opened wide. The two pieces of the broom were moving... and each piece was growing new arms and legs.

Faster than ever, the brooms
raced off for more water.
"I'm in big trouble now,"
thought Max, glumly.

In no time, the brooms
were back, sloshing water
everywhere.

Max tried to stop them.

He tried
tripping
them.

He even tried to sit on them.
But it was no use.

"I give up," said Max,
miserably. "Sticklewick is
going to be furious."

I wonder
what it's like to be
a tadpole...

Meanwhile, the brooms were
still dashing in and out, up and
down the steps. All the time,
the water was getting deeper.

Soon it reached Max's knees... then his waist... then his chest.

I wish I could swim.

SPLASH! SPLOSH! The brooms flung a few more pails of water into the room. Waves washed across the workshop.

Tabitha shot past, trying
to surf.

"I warned you not to try any spells," she spluttered, spitting out water. "Maybe next time you'll listen to me."

"If this goes on, there won't *be* a next time," muttered Max, desperately. "Help!" he yelled, climbing onto the table.

Somebody help!

But he knew there was no one around to hear.

Chapter 5

Sorcerer to the rescue

Suddenly, there was a loud
pop. Sticklewick appeared in
a shower of green sparks.

What on
earth...?

Before he could catch his breath...

...the two brooms flew down the steps and flung yet more water into the workshop.

40

"Galloping goblins!" cried the sorcerer. "What *has* that boy been doing?"

Quickly, he raised his wand and spoke the magic words.

Eye of bat and tooth of boar, return to how you were before!

In a flash, one of the brooms
vanished. The other whizzed
across the room and stood
neatly to one side.

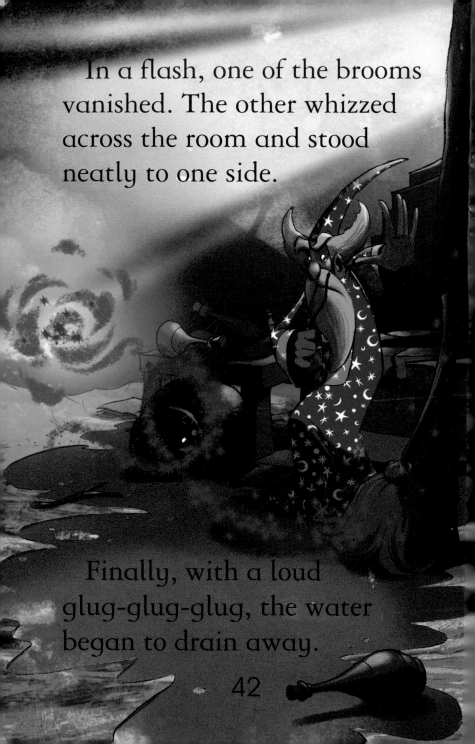

Finally, with a loud
glug-glug-glug, the water
began to drain away.

Nervously, Max climbed down from the table. His knees felt weak.

I'm in for it now.

Sticklewick glared at him. "Well? What have you got to say for yourself?"

43

"Um... I'm really sorry..."
"Not good enough!" roared
the sorcerer. "I warned you.
Now it's tadpole time."

Max dived behind the water
tank. "*Please* don't turn me into
a tadpole," he cried. "I won't
ever meddle with magic again."

"No, you won't," snapped Sticklewick. "Tadpoles can't do simple spells and they certainly can't do tricky ones..."

He paused and thought for a second. Max didn't dare move.

Hmm... that was quite a difficult spell you did...

Just then, Tabitha spoke. "He might be a good sorcerer one day... Maybe you should start teaching him magic."

He is your apprentice after all...

"Maybe..." said Sticklewick, "but first he cleans up here." He turned to Max. "And if you *ever* disobey me again, you'll be frogspawn in the moat."

From that day on, Max was a perfect pupil. Soon he learned how to do spells properly. And when he grew up, he became a great sorcerer...

...although he was always a little afraid of broomsticks.

The tale of *The Sorcerer's Apprentice* has been around for almost 2,000 years. It was first written down by a Greek named Lucian of Samosata. This version is based on a poem composed in 1797 by the German writer, Johann Wolfgang von Goethe.

Series editor: Lesley Sims
Designed by Katarina Dragoslavic

First published in 2007 by Usborne Publishing Ltd., Usborne House, 83-85 Saffron Hill, London EC1N 8RT, England. www.usborne.com Copyright © 2007 Usborne Publishing Ltd.
Printed in China. UE. First published in America in 2007.